IN THE NIGHT KITCHEN

MAURICE SENDAK

HARPER COLLINS PUBLISHERS

FOR SADIE AND PHILIP

DID YOU EVER HEAR OF MICKEY, HOW HE HEARD A RACKET IN THE NIGHT

AND SHOUTED

QUIET DOWN THERE!

AND THEY PUT THAT BATTER UP TO BAKE

A DELICIOUS MICKEY-CAKE.

SO HE SKIPPED FROM THE OVEN & INTO BREAD DOUGH
ALL READY TO RISE IN THE NIGHT KITCHEN.

HE KNEADED AND PUNCHED IT
AND POUNDED AND PULLED

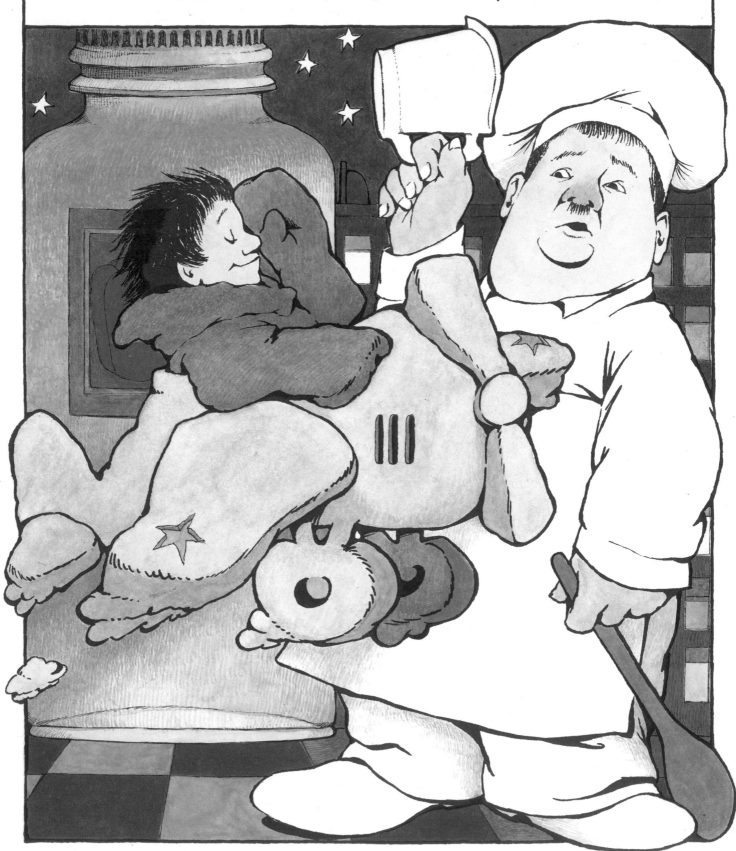

AND UP
AND UP

MICKEY THE MILKMAN DIVED DOWN TO THE BOTTOM

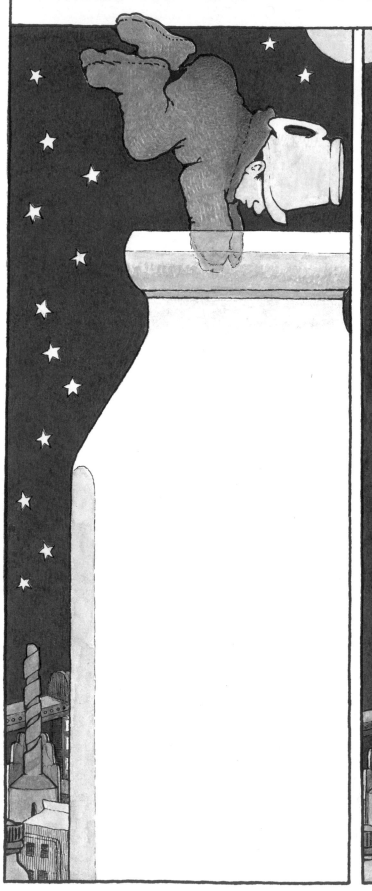

SO THE BAKERS THEY MIXED IT AND BEAT IT AND BAKED IT.